This
LazyTown Annual
belongs to

....

LAZY TOWN ™

Annual 2008

Contents

EGMONT

We bring stories to life

First published in 2007 in Great Britain by Egmont UK Limited
239 Kensington High Street, London W8 6SA

LazyTown © & ™ 2007 LazyTown Entertainment.
All related titles, logos and characters are trademarks of LazyTown Entertainment.
© 2007 LazyTown Entertainment. All rights reserved.

ISBN 978 1 4052 3184 8
3 5 7 9 10 8 6 4 2
Printed in Italy

"Hi, and welcome to **LazyTown!**

Robbie Rotten wants to make sure LazyTown is lazy, but we're not gonna let that happen, are we?

I'm ready for some fun and action! Are you? You are? Then let's GO FOR IT!"

Say hi to Sportacus

the all-action superhero!

Sportacus is an amazing, super-fit athlete and acrobat who loves to stay fit and active.

"No one's lazy in LazyTown!"

Sportacus eats lots of Sports Candy, the fruit and vegetables that give him energy. He also drinks lots of water. Did you know that water is called H_2O?

"That's what I call energy!"

Sportacus gets lots of sleep. It's his secret energy source. He always wakes up at sunrise.

Sportacus lives on a blue, red and white Airship packed with super-hi-tech equipment. He has a pedal-powered transporter called Skychaser and a mini plane called Fly Pod or Skutla. A special Crystal lets him know if someone's in trouble.

Copy colour
Sportacus

as neatly as you can, and write your name on the line.

Sportacus by

_____

"Go for it!"

Meet Robbie Rotten

Robbie Rotten is the world's laziest super-villain – and he wants everyone in LazyTown to be lazy, too.

Robbie's Lair is dark and creepy (just like him!) A purple periscope hangs from the ceiling and he uses it to keep his sneaky eyes on LazyTown.

Robbie's favourite pastime is being lazy. He spends as much time as he can lying in his orange fur recliner chair, trying to sleep.

Robbie's a master of disguise (well, he thinks he is). He keeps his disguises in glass cases.

"Let's keep LazyTown . . . lazy!"

Robbie's home is in an underground lair where he spends his time making plans that will stop Sportacus helping people stay active. Luckily, they never work.

Robbie likes:
- being lazy
- fluffy ear plugs
- junk food
- his orange fur recliner chair
- disguises

Robbie dislikes:
- Sportacus. "I really don't like him."
- Stephanie. "That pink-haired little girl."
- sports
- teamwork
- smiling – it makes his face hurt, so he doesn't do it often

Look out for Robbie Rotten!

Can you find 10 more of him, hiding on the pages in this Annual? Colour in an outline for each one you find, then write the page numbers in the boxes.

Check the answers on page 68.

"I'm just a simple Rotten guy."

Meet Stephanie

"There's always a way!"

Stephanie is a fun-loving, pink-haired eight year old who lives in LazyTown with her uncle, Mayor Milford Meanswell. She's made lots of friends and never wants to leave!

Stephanie is always on the go. Like Sportacus, she loves music, dancing, singing – **DOING!** She's full of ideas for new games, sports and adventures.

Stephanie tries to be positive and look on the bright side. Sometimes she's not sure whether to do the right thing or take the easy way out.

Stephanie's room is just like her: bright and colourful. It's her special place where she writes her secret diary, thinks, plans and dreams ...

Stephanie likes:

- Sportacus
- dancing
- singing
- pink

Stephanie dislikes:

- laziness
- giving up

"I feel like... dancing!"

Stephanie loves to surround herself with music.

Count the musical notes on this page and write a number in each flower.

1 2 3

Meet Ziggy

Ziggy is the youngest of the LazyTown kids. He's sweet and lovable, but eats too many sweets and candies. He just can't resist them!

"I'm Sportacandy!"

Ziggy loves to play, and he's always ready to say yes to a new idea or adventure. He likes to help out when he can.

Ziggy always wears his superhero costume. When he grows up he wants to be a superhero, just like Sportacus.

Ziggy loves lollipops!

How many is he holding? Circle the number.

1 2 3 4
5 6 7 8
9 10

ANSWER: 7 lollipops.

Meet

Stingy is six years old. He can be selfish, and doesn't like to share. He only does it when he has to.

Stingy is not a team player! Whatever is his is his, and whatever is yours is also his! He's a good guy deep down, but he keeps this well hidden.

Stingy's best friend is his piggy bank, where he keeps all his money!

Which piggy bank is the odd one out?

1

2

3

ANSWER: Piggy bank 2.

15

Meet

Pixel gets on better with computers than with people. He's more at home talking to screen-people. He's a whizz with gadgets.

Pixel is happiest in his room, glued to a screen and playing video games. He often stays up all night playing, then falls asleep during the day!

This is how Pixel writes the letter P.

Draw the first letter of **your** name as a Pixel-letter.

Pixel's house is ultra-hi-tech. The kids often meet there and hang out in his room, which is crammed with all sorts of games and gizmos.

"Coolness factor of plus five!"

Meet Trixie

Trixie is the natural leader of the kids. She's smart, and she knows it! She can solve problems quickly, and just can't help taking charge.

Trixie likes to do things FAST. She goes everywhere on her red and yellow scooter. She always wears her matching safety helmet, elbow and knee pads.

"Let's move it, people!"

Colour in Trixie's picture.

Do it as neatly as you can, but do it FAST, because she won't hang around for long!

Trixie loves jokes and playing tricks. She doesn't like rules, and usually ignores them!

17

Meet Milford Meanswell

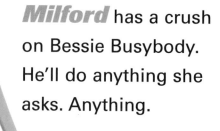

"Oh, my stars!"

Milford Meanswell is very proud to be the Mayor of LazyTown. He's Stephanie's uncle, and she's come to live with him.

Milford takes his job very seriously and always tries to do the very best he can. He does mean well, and likes being helpful.

Milford has a crush on Bessie Busybody. He'll do anything she asks. Anything.

Spot the difference

There are 3 things that are different in picture 2. Can you spot them?

1   2

ANSWERS: 1. Milford's coat patches are a different colour; 2. His tie is longer; 3. One of his coat buttons is missing.

Meet Bessie Busybody

"Oh, dear!"

Bessie Busybody is the LazyTown gossip. She has to know all there is to know about everyone. And she has to tell everyone what she knows. Bessie's favourite thing is her telephone.

Bessie thinks she's trendy, but her clothes are a bit out of date.

Bessie knows how keen Milford is on her. She knows if she hollers he'll come running.

As Milford says, "There's only one Bessie!"

Can you find the real Bessie?

1   2   3

Sportacus on the move

There's no such thing as a lazy day for an active superhero like Sportacus!

He wakes up at sunrise, stretches, and flips out of bed. The sports cupboard opens and he jumps out of his shoes and into a pair of roller blades. He does some spins, then grabs a hockey stick and shoots the pillow off the bed. He uses the stick to make his bed, then it folds into the wall! *Bed de-activated* says the Airship computer. *That's bed-making Sportacus style!*

Next it's time for the most important meal of the day, breakfast!

"Time for breakfast!"

Morning is when Sportacus gets his energy for the whole day. He calls fruits and vegetables Sports Candy. It's healthy and tastes good.

Sportacus loves melon and he has his own special way of eating it. He tosses a melon into the air, does some backflips, a handstand, then catches it before it hits the floor. *That's breakfast Sportacus style!*

"Mmm, I love melon."

When it's time to brush his teeth, Sportacus says, *"Toothbrush!"* and it shoots out of a slot in the wall. He brushes his teeth doing a backwards high-flip. *That's teeth-cleaning Sportacus style!*

"How much fun is it to brush your teeth?"

21

"Getting active is the best fun!"

Next it's time for Sportacus to get active. The Sports Spinner comes up from the floor and he spins its wheel. It helps him pick just the right activity, like Jumping Jacks.

When he's done, he spins the Sports Spinner again and pulls out another card. Power Jumping!

"1, 2, 3, 4, 5, 6, 7, 8, 9, 10 Power Jumps!"

Sportacus gets lots of mail. Letters go up a tube into the Airship. Some ask for help, like this one:

Dear Sportacus, ☺
Can you teach me to do one-armed push-ups?

Sportacus knows all about push-ups! He does normal ones, then one-armed ones! He does one-arm-one-leg push-ups, too!

"Lift one arm, and the opposite leg."

Sportacus always answers the letters kids send. He makes his replies into paper planes, and sends them flying through the sky. *That's sending mail Sportacus style!*

Sportacus always helps when anyone in LazyTown is in trouble. He needed all his strength when Ziggy got stuck up a tree one day!

Ziggy clung on to a branch, dangling in mid-air. "Help!" he cried. *"Heeeeeelp!"*

His screams were so loud that they woke Robbie Rotten in his underground lair.

"What's going on up there?" he said. "Can't a poor lazy man take a little nap without all this noise?"

Robbie looked through his periscope and saw Ziggy. "Couldn't he fall more quietly?"

Up on his Airship, Sportacus' crystal beeped a warning. "Someone's in trouble!" said Sportacus.

"Door!" he said, and the door to the platform opened.

"What's going on?"

"Someone's in trouble!"

24

Sportacus always tries to spot the problem before he leaves. He grabbed his telescope, looked into it – and saw Ziggy hanging from the tree branch.

Sportacus flipped into Skutla, pressed a button, and the Airship set off: **_whoooosh!_**

Sportacus grabbed one end of an extra-long scarf, jumped off the platform, and landed in LazyTown.

He grabbed a skateboard, lay flat on his back on it and rode it towards Ziggy.

But poor Ziggy couldn't hold on any longer. Suddenly, he lost his grip and fell!

"Heeeelp!"

Just in time, Sportacus slid under the tree branch and caught Ziggy in his arms!

Sportacus was checking that Ziggy wasn't hurt when his crystal beeped again. It was the start of a very busy day!

First Sportacus caught Stingy when Trixie jumped off the end of the see-saw and he flew up into the air ...

Next, Sportacus stopped Mayor Meanswell tripping over a skateboard and falling ...

Then he used a football to get an apple down from a tree for Stephanie ...

When it was time for Sportacus to leave he called for Skychaser.

"Gotcha!"

26

"It's time for bed now everyone in LazyTown is safe and happy," he said. "Well … almost everyone."

Sportacus hopped on to Skychaser and pedalled up to the Airship. "It's almost 8:08," he said. "Just in time to clean my teeth before bed. I have to get my sleep!"

Countdown to bedtime said the computer.

Sportacus flipped to his bed, dived under the covers and laid his head on the pillow.

It's the end of another Sportacus-style day. To be a superhero like him, you need to exercise, eat great, and sleep great. Then you're going to *feel* great.

"Goodnight, LazyTown!"

Go go kids!

Can you match the sports equipment to the sports?

1 *football*

2 *skateboarding*

3 *basketball*

4 *tennis*

ANSWERS: 1. b; 2. d; 3. a; 4. c.

Go for it!

Tick the sports you like to play.

cycling ☐

basketball ☐

netball ☐

swimming ☐

cricket ☐

football ☐

baseball ☐

skating ☐

bowling ☐

volleyball ☐

running ☐

tennis ☐

rugby ☐

skateboarding ☐

gymnastics ☐

Believe in yourself!

Sleepless in LazyTown

Up on his Airship, Sportacus said, "Almost 8:08. Time for bed." He snuggled in. "A good night's sleep will give me the energy I need tomorrow."

"It's easy!"

   Next morning, Stephanie was showing Sportacus how to play baseball.

   "It's easy," said Stephanie. "You throw the ball so I can't hit it, and I try to hit it as far as I can."

   Just then, Pixel arrived. "Sorry I'm late," he said. He took his place as catcher, but he soon fell asleep!

"Pixel, are you OK?" asked Stephanie.

"You were up all night playing video games again, weren't you?" said Ziggy. "Sportacus, don't you go to bed at 8:08?"

Sportacus nodded. "Sleeping's my secret energy source. When I get enough I can even learn a new sport – like baseball!"

Down in his lair, Robbie Rotten heard his words. "He gets his energy from sleeping, does he?" he cackled. "Then I'll make sure he doesn't get *any* sleep!"

He found a ball that made loud noises. "Let's see how much energy Sportacus has when this keeps him up all night!"

"Are you OK?"

"This will keep him awake!"

"Me!"

Back at the sports field, Pixel was still asleep.

"You be catcher, Sportacus, and I'll throw," said Stephanie. "But who will hit?"

Robbie arrived. "Me!" he said.

"You?" said Stephanie. "But you don't like sports."

"I can hit the ball further than anyone here," said Robbie, handing Sportacus the noise-ball. "How about it, Sportacus? A Rotten challenge! See you back here in two days. Whoever hits the ball furthest wins. And if I win, **you** leave LazyTown ... forever."

"How about a Rotten challenge?"

"Don't worry, Sportacus," said Stephanie. "We'll help you."

That night, the hands on Robbie's clock moved to 8:08. "Time for my noise-ball to wake Sportacus!" he laughed.

On the Airship, the noise-ball squeaked loudly and Sportacus woke up. It was the start of a long, sleepless night ...

"Time to wake Sportacus!"

When Sportacus got to the sports field next morning he lay down on a bench and fell asleep! Nothing woke him, not even Ziggy's ringing alarm clock!

"Brrrring!"

"You need sleep!"

Stephanie and Ziggy went to find Pixel. "You have to help Sportacus," Stephanie told him. "You need to throw so well that Robbie won't win. If he loses, Sportacus will have to leave LazyTown."

"Yes, you really need to sleep tonight," added Ziggy.

That night Pixel looked at his clock. "OK! Video games are good, but friends are better," he said. "Sportacus needs me to go to sleep right now, so I will."

"Sportacus needs me!"

That night, Sportacus was fast asleep ... when Robbie's noise-ball went off again. He flipped out of bed and grabbed it.

"So this is what's making the noises!" he said.

Next morning, Sportacus met Pixel at the sports field. He showed him the noise-ball.

"I found this," he said. "It's what kept me awake. Look, it says **Made in Robbie's Lair**."

"What can we do?" said Pixel.

"I have a plan ..." said Sportacus.

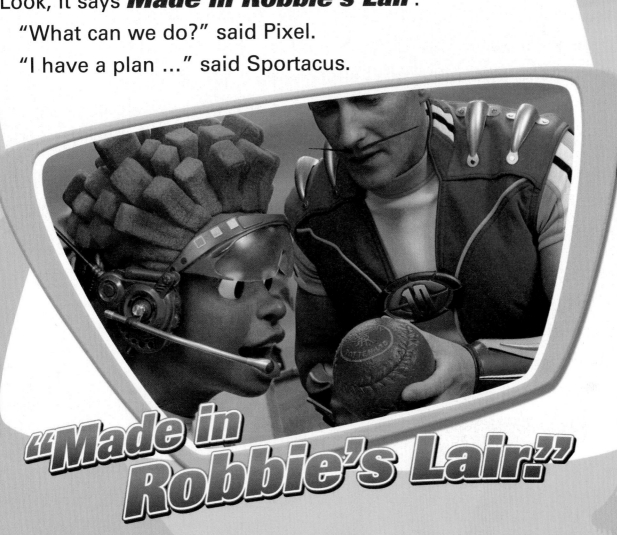

"Made in Robbie's Lair!"

When Robbie arrived at the sports field, Sportacus was lying on a bench. "Someone didn't get any sleep again last night!" laughed Robbie. "Come on, let's play."

"Throw!"

Pixel threw the first ball and Robbie missed it. He missed the second ball as well. He did hit ball number three, but it landed at his feet ...

"Your turn, Sporta-snore," said Robbie, but Sportacus pretended to be asleep! Robbie had to lift him up and put the bat into Sportacus' hands.

Pixel gave Robbie the noise-ball and he threw once, twice. Sportacus didn't move!

But when Robbie threw again, Sportacus opened his eyes. He hit the ball and it flew high into the air – and down into Robbie's Lair! Sportacus was the winner!

"Your turn, Sporta-snore!"

Robbie threw his cap to the ground and stormed off.

"Great throwing, Pixel!" said Sportacus.

"All I did was get some sleep!" said Pixel.

Sportacus smiled. **"Sleep is everything."**

"Sleep is everything."

Later, when Robbie was sleeping, a loud noise woke him up. It was his own noise-ball, the one Sportacus had hit into his lair!

"Nooo!" said Robbie. He'd been woken up by his own dastardly invention!

You can do it if you try!

"Sportacus says it's important to keep our bodies **and** our brains active, so give your brain a workout with this puzzle!"

38

Can you match the pictures to make pairs?

① **②** **③** **④** **⑤** **⑥**

Write a number next to each letter.

Which picture is left?

a ◯ **b** ◯ **c** ◯ **d** ◯ **e** ◯

ANSWERS: The pairs are: a – 3, b – 4, c – 1, d – 2, and e – 5. Number 6 is left.

39

Rotten Beard

One day, when Sportacus looked through his telescope to check on things in LazyTown, he saw Stephanie.

"Help!" she cried. *"Save me!"*

Sportacus went to help, but the kids were just playing pirates!

"A-harrrr! Pirate Stephanie be walkin' the plank!" said Trixie.

The kids made so much noise that Robbie heard it down in his lair. He saw them through his periscope. "Those rotten kids!" he said. "Noise, noise, nothing but noise!"

"Those rotten kids!"

The kids were still playing pirates when Mayor Meanswell arrived. "Do you know that LazyTown once had its own real-life pirate?" he said. "His story is in the LazyTown Big Book of History in my office. Come on, I'll show you!"

The Mayor opened the book and showed them a drawing of Rotten Beard the pirate!

"Rotten Beard took whatever he wanted from LazyTown," said the Mayor. "But the one thing he didn't take was the LazyTown Stone. The secret to living in LazyTown is carved on it. It's outside, I'll show you."

Robbie watched through his periscope, and listened ...

Rotten Beard

Mayor Meanswell showed the kids the LazyTown Stone. He read the words on it.

"LAZYTOWN SHOULD ALWAYS BE …" he said, then stopped. "The bottom of the stone is missing! When Rotten Beard couldn't have it, he broke it, and now that part is missing. People say it's buried in a pirate's treasure chest. If it's ever found we all have to do just what it says."

Robbie watched. "So if someone, meaning **ME**, made a fake stone, they'd all have to do whatever I wrote on it!" he said. "Time to put my carving skills to good use!"

Robbie soon made the fake stone piece. "Now to bury it where those kids will find it," he said, putting the stone in a treasure chest. *"Disguise time!"*

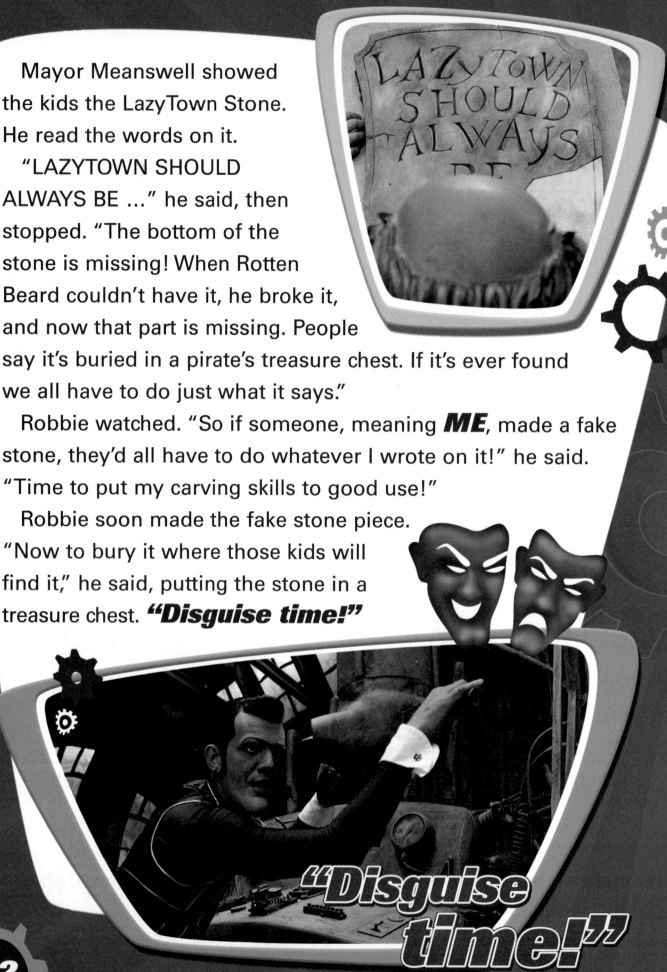

"Disguise time!"

At the Town Hall, the Mayor read more from the book. "The people couldn't stop Rotten Beard. But then one day a hero came to put an end to him and his lazy ways. They fought long and hard, and the hero defeated Rotten Beard. But he swore that one day, he would return."

When the kids went to look for the LazyTown Stone, they were surprised to meet a pirate riding along on a ship on wheels. It was Robbie, in one of his disguises!

"Avast, ye little buccaneers!"

"All aboard!"

"Avast, ye little buccaneers!" said the pirate. "If it's treasure ye seek, Rotten Beard has the map. Look, **X** marks the spot where the treasure be buried. I need ye puny pirates to help me find it! *All aboard!*"

Robbie took the kids to where he had buried the treasure chest. Stephanie dug down, and pulled out the chest. Inside was a broken piece of stone!

"The missing piece of the LazyTown Stone!" said Stephanie.

Stephanie sent a message to Sportacus: *We found the missing piece of the LazyTown Stone.*

"They found it!" said Sportacus. "Fantastic!"

Sportacus flew down to LazyTown as the Mayor fitted the little piece of stone into the big one. "LazyTown should always be …" he read. "What? … *LAZY*?"

"What does it mean?" asked Stephanie. "I don't understand."

"It means that everyone has to be *l-a-a-a-zy*!" said Pirate Robbie. "I'm going for a nap."

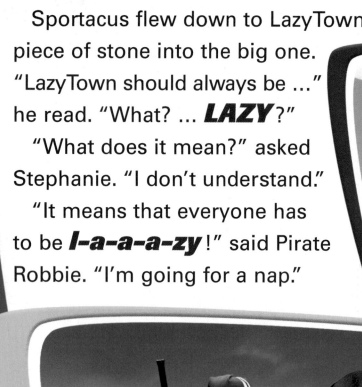

"What does it mean?"

"This is awful," said Stephanie. "I can't be lazy and do nothing all because of this stupid old stone!"

As she spoke, a secret compartment opened. "It's another treasure map!"

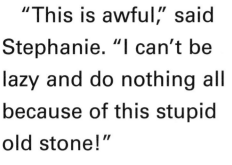

"It's another treasure map!"

"Help!"

The kids were soon busy digging again.

Pirate Robbie arrived as they pulled a **real** treasure chest out of the hole they'd dug!

This wasn't supposed to happen!

"Grrr!" said Robbie, before tying them to a tree!

"Take that!"

Sportacus heard the kids' cries for help, and rushed to the rescue.

When he arrived, Pirate Robbie turned on Sportacus.

After a struggle, Sportacus pushed him and Pirate Robbie fell into the hole the kids had dug!

"A hole in one!"

said Sportacus.

Robbie crawled out of the hole without his pirate hat and eye patch.

"Grrr!"

"That's no pirate!" said Stephanie. **"It's Robbie!"**

Sportacus untied the kids and opened the chest. Inside was the real missing piece of the LazyTown Stone!

The kids watched as he fitted it in place and read out the **real** message. "LazyTown should always be ... **HAPPY!**"

"Hurray!" said the kids.

"Hurray!"

"So all we have to do is **smile!**" said the Mayor.

"That's easy for you to say," said Robbie.

Later, in his lair, Robbie stood in front of a mirror and tried to smile.

The mirror cracked, and broke into a thousand pieces. **"Grrrrrrrrr!"**

"Smiling makes my face hurt!"

Disguise time!

Robbie Rotten calls himself the Master of Disguise. But Sportacus can always spot the real Robbie, thanks to his superhero observation skills.

Can **you** find the Robbie without a disguise? You have **2** minutes to find him.

1

2

4

3

5

6

7

8

9

10

Play Day

"Cool!"

At the Hangout, Ziggy slid down the slide. "That was cool! Your turn, Trixie!" he said.

Trixie slid down on her wagon. She whooshed past Ziggy, but couldn't stop! The wagon shot through town, out of control.

"Help!" cried Trixie as she headed for the LazyTown gate!

Up on the Airship, Sportacus' crystal beeped. "Someone's in trouble!" he said.

Down in his lair, Robbie was having his after-breakfast nap when Trixie's screams woke him. "What noisiness are those kids making now?" he said, looking through his periscope.

"I need my sleep!"

Sportacus flew down to LazyTown just in time to kick the gate open and stop Trixie and the wagon crashing into it.
Ziggy cheered. *"Great save, Sportacus!"*

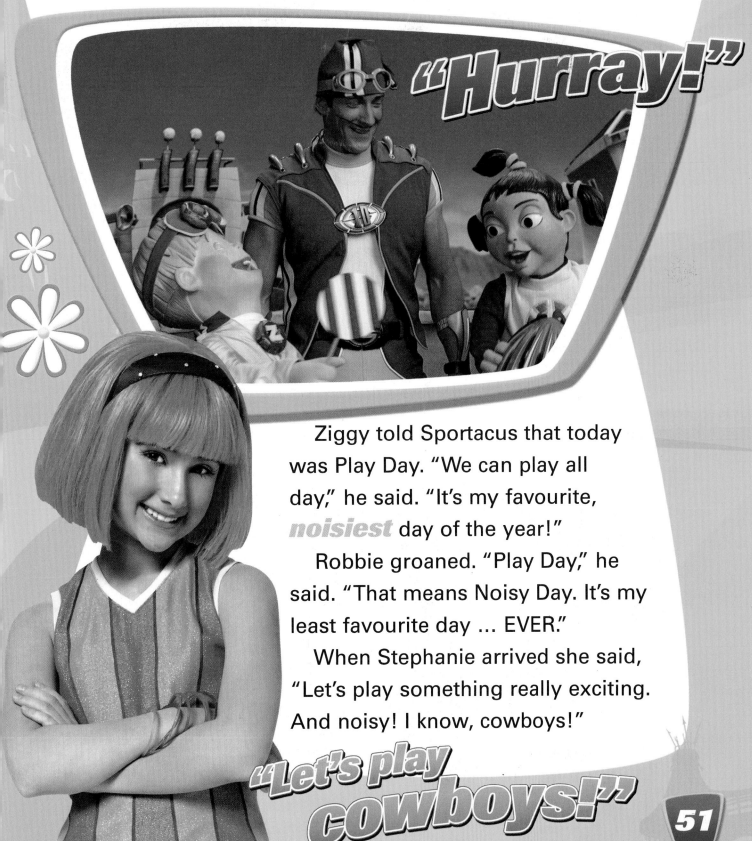

"Hurray!"

Ziggy told Sportacus that today was Play Day. "We can play all day," he said. "It's my favourite, *noisiest* day of the year!"

Robbie groaned. "Play Day," he said. "That means Noisy Day. It's my least favourite day … EVER."

When Stephanie arrived she said, "Let's play something really exciting. And noisy! I know, cowboys!"

"Let's play cowboys!"

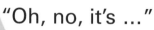

"Yippee-kay-yay!"

"Cowboys?" said Robbie. "That's way too noisy! I have to stop them or I'll never get any rest! **Disguise time!**"

Robbie pulled a lever and in a flash he was dressed as a cowboy. "Meet the Rotten Kid!" he said. "I'm gonna have a showdown with those kids. And when I win, they'll be quiet **forever**."

Back in the town, Sheriff Stephanie was facing up to Ziggy and Trixie when Cowboy Robbie appeared.

Ziggy gasped. "Who's that?" he said. "Oh, no, it's ..."

"Oh, no!"

"Say howdy to the Rotten Kid!"

"The Rotten Kid," said Cowboy Robbie, swinging a rope into a big loop. "And this town ain't big enough for the four of us."

Up on the Airship, Sportacus' crystal bleeped again. "Someone's in trouble!" he said.

He flew down to LazyTown and arrived just in time to see Cowboy Robbie roping the kids to a pole!

"Now that's what I call fancy ropin'!" said Cowboy Robbie. **"Help!"** cried Trixie.

"Help!"

Just then, Sportacus leapt into action. "Hold it right there!" he said, taking a ping-pong bat from his backpack and pointing it at Robbie. "Make your move."

"Sure will," said Robbie, pointing a candy cane at Sportacus. **"Draw!"**

"Apple!" shouted Sportacus, and an apple fell from the Airship. Sportacus used his bat to hit it at Robbie. It knocked his hat off and when he bent down to pick it up, Sportacus pushed him into a big bin.

"Bull's-eye!" said Trixie. "Thanks, Sportacus."

"Let's play something really wild next!" said Trixie.

"Wild animals," said Stephanie. "Let's get our costumes!"

"Bull's-eye! Thanks, Sportacus!"

54

Soon Stephanie was beating on a drum and roaring like a lion. *"SQUEAK!"* said Ziggy. "I'm a big wild ... mouse!"

"GRRR!" Trixie growled like a tiger.

Down in his lair, Robbie heard the kids making loud animal noises.

"So, they want to play wild animals, do they?" he said. "I'll show them a **really** wild animal!"

He pulled a lever, spun around, and was dressed in a gorilla costume!

Robbie picked up a banana. He was just about to take a bite when he stopped. "Yeuk!" he said. "No, I can't do it, even if I **am** a gorilla. Bananas are just too healthy!"

"Here comes son of Kong!"

Robbie found a gorilla mask. "Those kids are noisier than ever!" he said. "I'll have to **scare** them quiet."

Up in LazyTown, Robbie stood on a wall, banging his chest and making gorilla noises.

"It's a gorilla!" said Ziggy. *"Run!"*

"Whooooaa!" Robbie slipped off the wall, landed on a unicycle, and set off after the kids!

The unicycle was out of control! "How do I steer this thing?" yelled Robbie. "Help!"

Sportacus' crystal beeped. "Someone else is in trouble!" he said.

"Whoooaa!"

Down in LazyTown, Sportacus kicked a wheelbarrow in front of the unicycle to stop it. The gorilla flew up into the air and landed in it!

"Ouch!"

"Robbie Rotten!"

Sportacus pulled off the gorilla's mask. "This is no gorilla," he said. "It's Robbie Rotten!"

"I was just joining in with Play Day," moaned Robbie.

"Then you'll love playing our **BING BANG** song!" smiled Stephanie.

"My ears!" said Robbie. "I can't take it anymore!"

Let's move it!

"Getting active and moving around is good for you. Playing sports is a fun way to get active and stay active, and you can exercise anywhere!"

"I'm ready to go! Are you? Remember, no one's lazy in LazyTown - except Robbie!"

1 *"Warm up first. Stand with feet apart and clap your hands. 1, 2, 3, 4, 5, 6, 7, 8, 9, 10."*

2 *"Now stand with arms out to the side, and curl in. Repeat 9 more times."*

3 *"March on the spot. Count to 10. Remember to work those arms and legs!"*

4

"Now keep marching, but move your arms to the side, like this!"

5

"Do some jumps. Do 5, and try to get your legs higher each time. Great work!"

6

"Do some side stretches, 5 with the left leg, then 5 with the right."

"That was fun! Why not do it again, maybe with a friend this time? You could play some music as you move!"

7

"Always warm down after getting active. Stretch, and march on the spot."

One day, Sportacus met up with the kids at the Hangout.

"We're all in the Friends Forever club," said Ziggy. "Do you wanna join, Sportacus?"

"Sure!" said Sportacus. "But where's Stingy?"

"He's not in the club. He never wants to be part of a team," said Trixie.

"But he **is** our friend," said Stephanie. "I'll tell him he can join."

Just then the Mayor called a meeting. "Attention, everyone," he said. "Today is Treehouse Building Day! Teams will work together to build treehouses."

"Attention, everyone!"

Robbie watched from the back of the crowd. "Teams? Working together?" he said. **"Yeuk!"**

"Sportacus will help all the teams," said the Mayor. "He'll take a picture of each treehouse, and the winners will get this cup!"

"Oh, I want that cup," said Robbie lovingly. "When I win it, I'll be number one!"

"Great, guys!"

The kids got to work right away. They measured, sawed, hammered and painted, working as a team.

"We're doing great, guys," said Stephanie.

But Stingy didn't want to be part of the team. He wanted it to be **HIS** team. "My wood, my nails, remember?" he said. "So this is **my** treehouse, OK?"

"My treehouse, OK?"

Robbie didn't work in a team. He built his own treehouse, but it kept falling down …

"Time's up!" said the Mayor, but Robbie's treehouse was still in pieces.

"What? Already?" said Robbie. "I'm not finished."

Sportacus took photos of the kids and their treehouse … and Robbie and his wreck.

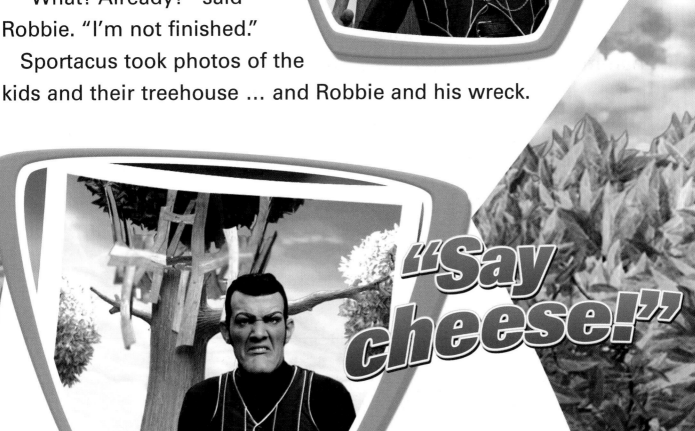

"Say cheese!"

The photos had to be posted to the judges.

Stingy took the kids' photo to the post box. But he tore off the others so he was the only one in the photo! "The trophy is mine!" he said.

Next day, the Mayor called another meeting. "The winning treehouse team is ... Stingy?" he said.

"NO!" said Robbie. "Not him! I want that cup!"

Trixie saw the torn photograph in the Mayor's hand. "How could you do that, Stingy?" she asked.

"My wood, my nails, my treehouse, my cup," said Stingy, running off to the treehouse.

"NO!"

"I don't need them!" he said. "I can have fun all by myself!"

But being on his own was no fun at all ...

"I don't need them!"

"Disguise time!"

Robbie still wanted the gold cup. **"Disguise time!"** he said, getting into the post box and shuffling off to the treehouse. Stingy was miserable on his own. But when he started to climb down from the treehouse, he slipped, and dangled in mid-air! "Help!" he cried. **"Heeeelp!"**

"Heeeelp!"

Sportacus saw Stingy through his telescope, and flew down to help.

The kids heard his cries, too, and they rushed to the treehouse to see if they could help.

Trixie climbed the tree and grabbed Stingy's hand.

"Be careful!" said Stephanie.

Just then Sportacus arrived on the rope ladder. He grabbed Stingy and Trixie and lowered them down to safety.

Creak! Crack! The treehouse wobbled, and started to fall towards the post box!

Sportacus caught it, and stood it back up again.

"Let me out!" said Robbie.

Sportacus picked up the post box and shook him out.

"Great teamwork!" said Sportacus.

"Great teamwork!"

"Thanks for saving me, Trixie," said Stingy.

"What are team-mates for?" said Trixie. "I know you really wanted that cup."

"I don't need a cup ... not when I have Friends Forever!"

"Mine at last!"

Later, Robbie sneaked off with the cup.

He polished and polished it until it shone like a mirror. Not many things make Robbie smile, but the cup did. He looked at it and smiled a big smile, but – **crack!** – it shattered into a thousand tiny pieces.

"No!" said Robbie. "Now I know why I don't like smiling!"

What do you know about LazyTown?

Now that you've met the characters, read the stories and had fun with the games, can you answer these questions?

1 I'm Mayor of LazyTown and Stephanie's uncle. Who am I?

2 Sportacus has a transporter that uses pedal-power. Is it called:

a Scooter

b Skychaser, or

c Swoosher?

3 In the story **Sleepless in LazyTown** on page 30, what did Robbie use to keep Sportacus awake?

4 Who wants to be a superhero called Sportacandy when he grows up?

5 What time does Sportacus go to bed? Is it:

a 8:28

b 8:18, or

c 8:08?

6 In the story **My treehouse** on page 60, what is the name of the kids' club?

7 Who rides around LazyTown on a red and yellow scooter?

8 Whose face hurts if he tries to smile?

Did you find all 10 Robbie Rottens?

He is on pages 17, 23, 29, 33, 39, 45, 49, 52, 58 and 65.

ANSWERS: 1. Milford Meanswell; 2. b, Skychaser; 3. A noise-ball; 4. Ziggy; 5. c, 8:08; 6. Friends Forever; 7. Trixie; 8. Robbie Rotten.

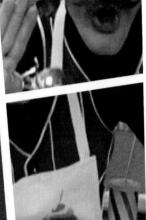
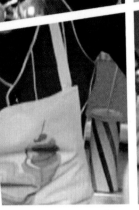